Praise for Marguerite Duras

"Marguerite Duras leads us into her characters with such grace and
power that we don't know what she's done until they take us over."
—Judith Rossner

"A spectacular success. . . . Duras is at the height of her powers."
—Edmund White

"The sentences lodge themselves slowly in the reader's mind until they
detonate with all the force of fused feeling and thought—the force of a
metaphysical contemplation of the paradoxes of the human heart."
—*New York Times*

"The descriptions are intriguing—every word counts. . . . But the book is
a pleasure to read, and even in translation the language is elegant."
—*People*

"Duras's writing has real power. Her strength is in her
images, in the music of her prose."
—*New Republic*

"Duras's language and writing shine like crystals."
—*New Yorker*

"Duras writes exquisitely . . . with a brilliant intensity
that is rare outside of poetry."
—*Daily Telegraph*

Select Books by Marguerite Duras in English Translation

The Sea Wall
The Sailor from Gibraltar
The Little Horses of Tarquinia
Whole Days in the Trees
The Square
Moderato Cantabile
Ten-Thirty on a Summer Night
Hiroshima Mon Amour
The Afternoon of Mr. Andesmas
The Ravishing of Lol Stein
The Rivers and the Forests
The Vice-Consul
L'Amante Anglaise
Destroy, She Said
India Song
Eden Cinema
The Man Sitting in the Corridor
Green Eyes
Agatha
Outside
Savannah Bay
The Malady of Death
The Lover
The War
Blue Eyes, Black Hair
Practicalities
Emily L.
Summer Rain
The North China Lover
Yann Andrea Steiner
No More

Introduction by Kazim Ali
Afterword by Sharon Willis

L'Amour
Marguerite
Duras

Translated from the French
by Kazim Ali and Libby Murphy

OPEN LETTER
LITERARY TRANSLATIONS FROM THE UNIVERSITY OF ROCHESTER

Library of Congress Cataloging-in-Publication Data:

Duras, Marguerite.
   [L'Amour. English]
   L'Amour / by Marguerite Duras ; translated from the French by
Kazim Ali and Libby Murphy. — First edition.
     pages cm
   ISBN-13: 978-1-934824-79-5 (pbk. : acid-free paper)
   ISBN-10: 1-934824-79-8 (pbk. : acid-free paper)
   I. Ali, Kazim, translator. II. Murphy, Libby, translator. III. Title.
   PQ2607.U8245A6513 2013
   843'.912—dc23
                     2012044429

Printed on acid-free paper in the United States of America.

Text set in Caslon, a family of serif typefaces based on the designs of
William Caslon (1692–1766).

Design by N. J. Furl

Open Letter is the University of Rochester's nonprofit, literary translation press:
Lattimore Hall 411, Box 270082, Rochester, NY 14627

www.openletterbooks.org

Introduction
by Kazim Ali

L'Amour, never before translated into English, is at the heart of a constellation of texts, both verbal and visual, by Marguerite Duras, sometimes called the India cycle. It was preceded by the more conventionally plotted and written novels *Le Ravissement de Lol V. Stein* and *Le Vice-Consul* and followed by the films *La Femme du Gange* (adapted from *L'Amour*) and *India Song* (adapted from *The Vice-Consul*), remade with different visuals the following year as *Son nom de Venise dans le Calcutta desert*. Like the sea which serves as its backdrop, the novel *L'Amour* repeats, concludes, and originates characters and themes that dream themselves both forward and back from its writing.

The continuity of characters from novel to novel and then into the films is never fully certain, as if Duras meant the reader to be unsure who these characters are or if these works are intended as true sequels. For example, the character of Michael Richardson from

The Ravishing of Lol Stein (as the title was translated) reappears in Duras's mythic Calcutta of *The Vice-Consul*, but is called Michael Richard. In *India Song* he has once more become Michael Richardson. The characters in *L'Amour* are unnamed, but when Duras transformed the novel into the screenplay for *La Femme du Gange,* she called the woman sitting on the beach "L.V.S." in the shooting script, though in the film itself she remains unnamed. The character of the traveler is named in the film as Michael Richardson. The making of *La Femme du Gange* also lead directly, according to Duras, to the film version of *India Song,* in which the story of Anne-Marie Stretter (and somewhat obliquely, the story of Lol) concludes. In *L'Amour* the woman on the beach drifts in and out of clarity. By *La Femme du Gange,* L.V.S. is more clearly portrayed as insane; in *India Song,* she merges with the madwoman of Calcutta in *The Vice-Consul* and disappears into incomprehensibility.

Places are similarly clouded. In *The Vice-Consul* Calcutta is a walkable distance from Lahore; Duras was quite familiar with South Asian geography, so one must understand these places as somewhat symbolic. Similarly, the characters' last names themselves (Stein, Karl, Stretter, Hold, Richardson) in the French text offer a feeling of geographical placelessness, neither feeling like a French locale, nor a Vietnamese one, though the river and island described in *L'Amour* evoke the Mekong River of Duras's childhood. The town where Lol lives is called S. Tahla in *The Ravishing of Lol Stein* (mistranslated in the English version as "South Tahla") and is far from T. Beach, the beachside town where Lol is going at the end of that book, but in *L'Amour* the town is called S. Thala (slightly different spelling) and lies on the beach itself.

L'Amour is also the last novel Duras wrote until 1984's *The Lover.* During the thirteen years in between she focused mainly on film, though she did publish several short prose narratives and a book of essays originally written as a column for a French newspaper. The text of *L'Amour* is highly poetic, fragmented, cinematic, visual, and strangely paced. It was as if with *L'Amour* Duras came to the edge of possibilities of book-length fiction and turned fully to embrace film. The character Lol V. Stein may have, in fact, a secret origin in film. In 1964, Anaïs Nin's agent sent Duras, the lauded screenwriter of 1959's *Hiroshima Mon Amour*, a copy of Nin's novel *A Spy in the House of Love* (1961) in the hopes that Duras would adapt the book for film. Nin flew to France and had a cordial visit with Duras. But later that summer when Duras's script arrived in New York, Nin was disappointed: "It is a Marguerite Duras story. It is not Sabina." Later, Nin would express disappointment that her "sexually liberated" Sabina was converted by Duras into a "schizoid" and a "whore." The film, which would have paired Duras's script with Joseph Losey's directing, was never made. The following year Duras published *Le Ravissement de Lol V. Stein,* a work that launched her into a decade-long exploration in fiction and film of sexuality, love, desire, rejection, and abandonment. *A Spy in the House of Love* seems to have inspired *Le Ravissement de Lol V. Stein* and also *L'Amour* in various ways: a woman struggling to define herself and her relationship to sexuality, the beach setting, the character of the male voyeur, the man with a piercing blue gaze wandering along the wrack line, and the by now iconic Duras scene of a recumbent woman, her eyes closed, being watched by a man.

Ironically, it was the film version of *The Lover* that led Duras back to both an experimental prose (after four other more conventionally written novels written after *The Lover*) and to her mode of revisiting earlier stories. Dissatisfied with the way the *The Lover* was adapted to the screen, she wrote a new version of that story called *The North China Lover* that returned to the fragmented and self-referential film-novel style of *L'Amour*.

But the woman in *L'Amour* is more than Lol V. Stein; she is all of Duras's madwomen distilled into one. She occupies a completely blank canvas—the beach and eerily empty streets of S. Thala—completing one corner of the strange triangle that comprises the heart of the narrative and dramatic action of the book.

It's easy to see how the writing of *L'Amour* would lead Duras into filmmaking. Its odd detachment, disembodiment, and notational qualities find full flowering in the films Duras made in the decade following its publication, and in the screenplays for those films, wonderful literary documents in and of themselves. As a written text it is strange, spare, poetic, brilliant and perhaps ahead of its time with its contradictory chorus of voices and its monochromatic mood. The starkness of tone and flatness of delivery may be why it has not yet been translated into English. But it leans toward film also in its sometimes self-conscious performativity. The characters themselves move, as if on a stage, before one another as audience. They watch. They are watched. They listen. They are heard. And sometimes fall silent, wander "off-stage," into the town or beyond the sea wall.

The stillness of the text and the static nature of its characters is a deception—in fact it is full of movement, people shifting from place to place, endlessly moving with the rich palette of variation in verbs that only French can provide: *venir, partir, revenir, repartir, marcher, aller, traverser, se promener,* and so on. The text itself stutters and stammers with endless repetitions that often slow down and compartmentalize the action; it is spare, but anything but elegant. It stumbles, often awkwardly, around a series of repeated actions.

The characters themselves wander through the novel, often with amnesia, not remembering each other or earlier events. Since the characters are unnamed, there are many moments when it is hard to know who is who. A woman shows up mid-novel at the hotel of the traveler, and for some pages it is hard to sort out whether she is the woman from the beach or the woman from the town. Eventually we understand her to be a third woman, the wife of the traveler. Some of these issues of identification and relation between characters are cleared up and made more obvious by Duras in the film script of *La Femme du Gange,* but while the woman who shows up at the voyager's hotel is clearly noted in the script as a third, different woman, *she is played by the same actress* who plays the woman in the house in the town of S. Thala.

We tried to find equivalences in tone when we could not find equivalences in language. Duras's text is the body of an other: strange, sometimes uneven, often awkward and unfamiliar. We tried not to smooth too much out. Recognizing the way Duras's tendency to use commas to string endless thoughts together can imitate the lull and ebb of the sea, we worked not to over-Anglicize syntax; as a result the text may retain some of the French sentence structure. When Duras gave no context for actions or locale, we restrained from a translation that would impart information.

Character here is subtle, fine-tuned, strange. Plot is ghostly and barely relevant. The forward momentum of the story is in breath, in anticipation, in fear, in lust—in fact, though Duras herself commented that the title of the book may have been a particularly brutal joke, *L'Amour* is a masterful study of longing, desire, denial, and desperation—in other words, of love; more than forty years after it was first published it is as disturbing as ever.

In the cool summer night after a rainstorm, the wind blowing through my room, the white curtains blowing in the wind, wind across my bed, it's late. I should be asleep. Instead I sit with a novel of sentences, in which the past is a barely visible ghost haunting everything, a novel in which the sounds of devouring desire haunt everything, a song from long ago, heard from behind a closed door, drifts through still, a novel, like the curtains, which quivers in the wind.

—KA, Oberlin

L'Amour

A man.

Standing, watching: the beach, the sea. The sea is calm, flat; season indefinite, moment lingering.

The man stands on a boardwalk over the sand.

He wears dark clothes. His face distinct.

His eyes clear.

He does not move. He watches.

The sea, the beach, a few tidal pools, flat surfaces of water.

Between the man who watches and the sea, far off, all the way at the water's edge, someone walking. Another man. Wearing dark clothes. From here his face is indistinct. He walks, going, coming, he goes, comes again, his path is rather long, never changing.

Somewhere on the beach, to the right of the one who watches, a movement of light: a pool empties, a spring, a stream, many-mouthed streams, feeding the abyss of salt.

To the left, a woman with closed eyes. Sitting.

The man who walks looks nowhere, looks at nothing, nothing but the sand in front of him. His pace is steady, unceasing, distant.

The triangle is completed by the woman with closed eyes. She is sitting against the wall that separates the beach from the town.

The man who watches is between this woman and the man who walks along the edge of the sea.

Because of the man who walks, constantly, with his slow, even stride, the triangle stretches long, reforms, but never breaks.

This man has the even steps of a prisoner.

·

Day dwindling.

The sea, the sky, fill the space. Far off, the sea, like the sky, already oxidized by the shadowy light.

Three, three in the shadowy light, a slow-shifting web.

·

The man is still walking, coming, going, before the sea, the sky, but the man who was watching has moved.

The even sliding of the triangle ceases.

He moves.

He begins to walk.

·

Someone walks, nearby.

The man who was watching passes between the woman with closed eyes and the other, far away, the one who goes, who comes, a prisoner. You hear the hammering of his steps on the boardwalk. His steps are uneven, hesitant.

The triangle comes undone, reforms. It comes apart. The man passes. You see him, you hear him.

You hear: his pace slacken. The man must be looking at the woman with closed eyes sitting before him.

Yes. The steps stop. He looks at her.

Only the man who walks along the sea continues his movement, his unending prisoner's pace.

The woman is watched.

She sits with her legs stretched out. She is in the shade, huddled against the wall. Eyes closed.

Unaware of being seen. Not knowing she is being watched.

Facing the sea. Blank expression. Hands half-buried in the sand, still, like her body. Strength sapped, shifted toward absence. Stopped short. Not knowing. Unaware.

•

The steps resume.

Uneven, hesitant, they resume.

They stop again.

Again resume.

The man who was watching has gone by. His steps fade. He can be seen, he walks toward a sea wall between the woman and the one who walks along the shore. Past this sea wall, another town, and farther still, distant, another town, blue, begins to blink with electric lights. Then other towns, more, more of the same.

He comes to the sea wall. He does not pass it.

He stops. Sits.

He sits on the sand, facing the sea. He ceases to see any of it, the beach, the sea, the man who walks, the woman with closed eyes.

For one moment, no one watches, no one is seen:

neither the mad prisoner who is still walking along the shore, nor the woman with closed eyes, nor the seated man.

For a moment, no one listens, no one hears.

And then there is a cry:

the man who was watching closes his eyes, seized by a feeling that lifts him, lifts him up, lifts his face up to the sky, his face contorts, and he cries out.

•

A cry. Someone cried out over by the sea wall.

The cry uttered and heard throughout space, whether occupied or empty. It has torn the shadowy light, the stillness. The steps of the man who walks have not stopped, have not slowed,

but she, she lifts her arm slightly, like a child, covers her eyes, stays like this a couple of seconds,

and he, the prisoner, this motion, he has seen it: he has turned his head in the direction of the woman.

•

Her arm lowered now.

The story. It begins. Began before the walk along the edge of the sea, the cry, the gesture, the movement of the sea, the movement of the light.

But now it becomes visible. It is already tracing itself onto the sand, on the sea.

The man who was watching returns.

Again his steps are heard, he is seen returning from the direction of the sea wall. His pace is slow. His gaze distracted.

As he approaches the boardwalk, a rising noise, cries, cries of hunger. Seagulls. They are there, were there, all around the man who walks.

The steps of the man who was watching.

He passes before the woman. He comes within range of her. He stops. He looks at her.

We will call this man the traveler—if there is need—because of the slowness of his stride, the distractedness of his gaze.

•

She opens her eyes. She sees him, looks at him.

He comes closer to her. He stops. He has reached her.

He asks:

–What are you doing here, night is falling.

She replies, very clearly:

–I'm looking.

She gestures before her, the sea, the beach, the blue town, the white roofs beyond the beach, everything.

He turns: the man who walks along the shore has disappeared.

He takes another step, leans against the wall.

He is there, next to her.

The intensity of the light changes, is changing.

It grows white, changes, is changing. He says:

–The light is changing.

She turns slightly toward him, she speaks. Her voice is clear, so gentle and mild, nearly frightening.

–You heard someone cry out.

Her tone does not invite response. He responds:

–I heard.

She turns back to the sea.

–You arrived this morning.
–Yes.

The pattern of her thought is clear. She gestures around her, the space, she explains:

–This—this is S. Thala, all the way to the river.

She is silent.
The light changes again.
He raises his head, looks in the direction of her gesture: he sees that from the far end of S. Thala, toward the south, the man who walks is returning, making his way through the seagulls, he is returning.
His pace is even.
Like the changing of the light.

Accident.

Again the light: the light. Changes, then suddenly does not change anymore. Brightens, freezes, even, shining. The traveler says:

–The light.

She looks.

The man who walks has reached the point in his walk where he had stopped a moment earlier. He stops. He turns, he sees, he too looks, he waits, he looks again, he starts again, he comes.

He comes.

His footsteps cannot be heard at all.

He arrives. He stops opposite the one who leans against the wall, the traveler. His eyes are blue, piercing, transparent. The emptiness in his gaze is absolute. He speaks with a firm voice, gesturing around him, everywhere. He says:

–What's happening here?

He adds:

–The light has frozen.

His tone expresses violent hope.

Light frozen, shining.

They look all around them at the flood of light, shining. The traveler speaks first:

–It will shift again.
–You think?
–I think so.

She is silent.

He approaches the traveler leaning against the wall. His eyes fix on him, blue, engulf him. The man gestures with his hand, points beyond the sea wall.

–You're staying at the hotel over there?
–Yes. I arrived this morning.

She is silent, still watching the frozen light. He takes his eyes off the traveler, notices the stillness of the light.

–Something is bound to happen. This is impossible.

Silence: with the light, sound also has ceased, the sound of the sea.

His blue gaze comes back to focus upon the traveler:

–This isn't the first time you have come to S. Thala.

The traveler tries to answer, several times he opens his mouth to respond.

–Well—you see—he stops.

His voice has no echo. The stillness in the air equals the stillness of the light.

He tries to answer.

They don't expect a response.

Unable to respond, the traveler raises his hand and gestures at the space around him. Finally, he manages to come closer to an answer:

–Well—he stops—I remember, yes, I remember–

He stops.
Her luminous voice rises up to him with dazzling clarity, she asks:

–What?

An uncontrollable shudder, from within, overwhelming, leaves him breathless. He whispers:

–All of it. Everything.

He has answered:
the movement of the light resumes, the sounds of the sea resume, the blue gaze of the man who walks recedes.
The man who walks gestures at everything, the sea, the beach, the blue town, the white capital, he says:

–Here, this is S. Thala, until the river.

His movement stops. Then his movement resumes, he gestures again, but more precisely, it seems, at all of it, the sea, the beach, the blue town, the white town, towns beyond, others still: all the same. He adds:

–And after the river, that's S. Thala as well.

He leaves.

She gets up. She follows him. Her first steps are unsteady, very slow. Then they even out.

She walks. She follows him.

They move away.

They skirt S. Thala, it seems; they do not enter its depths.

Dusk falls.

•

Night.

The beach and the sea are in darkness.

A dog passes, going toward the sea wall.

No one walks on the boardwalk, but, on the benches lining it, people sit. They relax. Are silent. Separated from one another. They do not speak.

The traveler passes. He walks slowly, he goes in the same direction as the dog.

He stops. Returns. He seems to be out for a walk. He starts off again.

His face is no longer visible.

The sea is calm. No wind.

The traveler returns. The dog does not return. The sea begins to rise, it seems. Its sounds getting closer. Muffled thudding coming from the river's many mouths. Somber sky.

•

Night still.

The traveler is seated facing an open window in a room. Sitting in the electric light. What lies beyond the window on this side of the hotel cannot be seen.

Night outside.

It is not the sea that is heard. The room does not look out on the sea. An incessant gnawing sound, muted, pervasive.

The man takes a piece of paper, he writes: *S. Thala. S. Thala. S. Thala.*

He stops. He seems to hesitate between each written word.

He begins again. Slowly, with certainty, he writes: *S. Thala, 14 September.*

He underlines the first word. Then he writes:

Don't bother coming there's no point.

He pushes the letter away, stands up.

He paces up and down the room.

He lies down on the bed.

The traveler, the man in the hotel.

Lying on the bed in the electric light, he turns to face the wall, you cannot see his face anymore.

Far off, through the deep gnawing, in the thick darkness, police sirens wail.

Then nothing but the gnawing in the darkness.

•

Day.

Once more, the man walking along the shore.

She is there, once again, against the wall.

The light is intense. She is completely still, her lips clamped shut. Pale.

On the beach, a certain energy of life.

She makes no sign at all at the approach of the traveler.

He walks to the wall, sits next to her. He looks at what she wants, it seems, to avoid seeing: the sea, the nauseous movements of swelling, the seagulls that cry out and devour a carcass on the sand, its blood. She says slowly:

–I'm pregnant, I feel like I'm going to vomit.
–Don't look there, look at me.

She turns toward him.

Far off, there, the man stops in the midst of the seagulls. Then moves again, toward the sea wall. She asks:

–Have you been here long?
–Yes.

She sits facing the sand. He looks toward the sea wall, at the man who is walking away.

–Who is he?

She pauses briefly, answers:

–He takes care of us. He watches over us. Brings us back.

He watches him for a while.

–His path is always the same, his pace so regular, you'd think–

She shakes her head: no.

        –No, it's the rhythm of this place, she says. The
        rhythm of S. Thala.

They wait.
The surface of the sea, still swelling, the fever.

        –Have you tried to throw up?
        –It won't help, it'll start again.

Waiting still.
The light begins to fade.
The first seagulls leave the beach, flying toward the sea wall.
The man who walks does not return their way: he goes up toward
S. Thala. He does not go in. He disappears behind the sea wall. You
no longer see him.
The traveler says:

        –We're alone?

She shakes her head:

        –No.

Waiting.
More gulls launch in white bursts.
Fly off.
Their departure quickening.
The traveler says:

–You can look now.

She looks up cautiously: the movement of the waves visible again, the swelling surface dispersing in white bursts. He says:

–The color is gone.

The color has disappeared.
Then the movement too.
The last gulls are gone. The sand, once again, covers the beach. He says:

–There's nothing left.

He listens to her, she breathes, she shifts, watches, for a long time she observes the coming shadows, the sand. Then, once more, she is still.
She listens, she hears, she says:

–There's noise.

He listens. Finally he hears something: he thinks it is the ebb and flow of the sea, the water crashing back into the abyss of salt. He says:

–It's the waves.
–No, she stops. It's coming from S. Thala.
–What is it?
–S. Thala. The sound of S. Thala.

He listens again for a while. He recognizes the incessant gnawing. He says:

–They're eating.

She doesn't know exactly. She says:

–They're going home—or sleeping, or nothing.

They are silent, they wait in silence for the sounds of S. Thala to cease.

The noise seems to ebb. Again she breathes.

Shifts.

She looks at him, the traveler, she looks at his clothing, his face, his hands. She touches his hand, grazing it tentatively, lightly, then she points toward the sea wall:

–The cry came from over there.

From the direction she points, he suddenly reappears.

Still very far off.

From the sea wall, he returns, the one who walks. There he is.

Behind him, the sea rises, an unending chain of lights blink on. Beyond the lights, clouds of smoke from refineries, dark.

He arrives, walking along the edge of the sea, staring ahead vacantly. She points him out to the traveler:

–He's coming back.

He looks:

–Coming back from where?

She peers in the direction he came from, the one who walks, she declares:

–Sometimes he walks past S. Thala and you just have to know . . . to wait.

Far off, he continues to come toward them, he cuts across the beach in their direction. The traveler says:

–You can't go past S. Thala, you can't get there.
–No, but he—she stops. –Sometimes he gets lost.

He comes. They wait for him.
He arrives. He is there. He looks at them. He sits, is silent, his blue gaze inspecting the space around him, then he speaks, he tells them very clearly:

–We were wrong. The cry came from farther away.

They wait: he says nothing more.

–From where?
–From everywhere. He stops. –There were so many of them. Millions. He stops again. –Everything is ravaged.

He looks at her. He points:

–Has she tried to vomit?

The traveler responds:

–It won't help, it'll just start again.
–True.

She is the first to rise. She rises.
She stands. Leans against the wall.
After a little while, they also rise.
They are all standing.
The traveler gestures at the sea before them, the sea and then behind them, the depths:

–What are you doing? Walking along the shore?
Next to S. Thala?
–Yes.
–Nothing else?
–No.

His blue gaze returns to the sea. Clear, focused, intense. The traveler says:

–And yet . . . this movement so clear, so regular
. . . this path so precise . . .
–No. No . . . he pauses—no . . . —he pauses
again—I'm mad.

They look at each other, they look, wait. The wind comes in, passes over S. Thala. The blue eyes monitor the sky, the sea, every movement, with the same attention.

The first to move away, to break the stillness, is the man who walks. His pace even as soon as he starts to walk.

She follows him. Her steps are unsteady at first, very slow. Then more even. She walks the way he leads. She lags behind.

So he pauses to let her catch up. She catches up.

Then he resumes his walk, toward the river. She catches up. He continues. This must be the way they cover the distance, every day, the expanse of the sands of S. Thala.

They disappear, turn along the river. They skirt, avoid, do not enter the depths of stone.

•

Three days.

Three days, during which there is a Sunday. The sound grows, S. Thala reels, then the sound fades away.

A storm comes that unsettles the sea.

Three nights.

In the morning, dead gulls on the beach. Over by the sea wall, a dog. The dead dog lies facing the pillars of a bombed-out casino. Above the dead dog, the sky is very dark. It is after the storm, the sea is rough.

The spot of wall is empty, the wind lashes against it.

The sea carries away the dead dog, the seagulls.

The sky grows calm. The unending chain emerges from the refineries. Then the sea. The sun.

•

Sun. Evening.

With the evening she reappears. She arrives on the boardwalk. Behind her, the one who walks.

They have both returned. They come from the river, cross S. Thala, walk from one end to the other. They are coming out of three days of darkness, once again they are seen in the sunlight of a deserted S. Thala.

The traveler steps out of the hotel behind the wall, sees them, approaches them.

Behind her, the other stops as soon as the traveler leaves the hotel; she moves forward. She has not yet seen the traveler coming to meet her. She moves forward, driven by the will of the one who is stopped behind her.

They have reached one another. She sees the traveler, almost does not recognize him.

She recognizes him.

Behind her, the other one turns around, starts off again. He has set off again toward the river.

She says:

−Ah, you came.

The storm has deepened her features.

They head first toward the sea wall, then toward the river, they stop, walk again, go toward a bright light on the boardwalk, at the edge of the sea, at the edge of the sands, before the depths, the unending chain of stone.

They watch the light for a long time.

Then they go in.

She is hungry.

She eats, watches, listens. There are things to see, to hear, streams of words, words, laughter. He watches with her, but in a different way, occasionally turning and looking at her. She says:

–I'm hungry, I'm expecting a child.

When she says it her gaze intensifies then fades just as quickly— she repeats:

–A child.
–Again?
–Yes.
–Whose is it?

She doesn't know.

–I don't know

She smells of sand, of salt. The storm has deepened the circles under her eyes.

The noise of the café grows. When the noise grows too loud her eyes open painfully. Her attention wanders. She asks:

–You come every day to S. Thala.
–Yes.
–It's far—she adds—it's a long distance, isn't it?
–Yes.

He tries to see beyond the walls, beyond the panes of glass.

She is here watching, in the confined space.

Beyond the windows, past the boardwalk, beyond the beach, someone goes by, a shadow walks at a steady pace, heads straight for the black expanse of the sea wall. The traveler follows him with his eyes for a long time, until he disappears into darkness. He says:

–He just walked off, didn't even look around.

She says clearly:

–He's searching—she adds—we must let him be.

She sees that he is next to her—the traveler, the man from the hotel. She raises her hand, touches his face, touches the skin softly while her voice swells forth, echoless.

–Why did you come back to S. Thala?

They look at each other.

–It's about a trip I wanted to take.—he stops.

They look at each other again, then his face turns away, her hand falls.
They sit there without speaking.
For a long time.
The noise fades.
The place empties.
They stare straight ahead, listening. For a long time.
The noise fainter still. It is as if she is expecting an ending, the threat of which seems to grow as the noise fades. She says:

–They're leaving.

–Who are they?

She points within the space, beyond the windows, everywhere, the unending chain of flesh. Her gesture is open, desperately tender:

–My people, the people of S. Thala.

Here, the noise has ceased. Over there, the incessant gnawing resumes, grows.
Changes.
It turns into singing. A distant singing.
The people of S. Thala are singing.
She looks around her, in front of her:

–They're gone—she listens—do you hear them?

Their eyes wander, gaze past the windows, they listen to them singing. They listen to the distant singing. She raises her hand:

–Do you hear?—she pauses—It's that music.

It is a slow march with solemn undertones. A slow dance, of parties long past, wild feasts.
She doesn't move. She listens to the distant hymn. She says:

–I have to sleep or I'm going to die.

She points in the direction where she sleeps.

–I have to cross the river—she stops.

She listens.

He is afraid: she is not moving, she is no longer breathing, she is listening to that music. He asks:

–Who are you?

The music continues. She replies:

–The police have a number.

The music continuing still. She looks at him:

–Why are you crying?
–Am I crying?

The door opens with a blast of wind.
The man who walks.
Here he is.
He enters, alone, the door closes behind him. All of a sudden, with him: the iodine of the sea, the salt, the searing blue intensity of the eyes of full daylight, full of night.
He straightens, listens to the faraway dance, says:

–Do you remember? The music of S. Thala.

Attentive, he listens. A blissful smile sweeps across his face. He listens intently, with extravagant gravity, to the distant music.
She points to the traveler, says:

–He's crying.

The blue eyes also fill with tears. His smile remains fixed. He explains:

–The music of S. Thala makes me cry.

The music stops.
He strains to hear it. He gives up.
The gnawing begins again, the silence.
She says, pointing to the traveler:

–He was afraid.
–Of what?
–Of not seeing you again.
–It is true that . . .

The blue eyes stare, see again. See the danger, the destruction.

–It's true that I got lost over there, I went too far—he adds—too long.

He points down the lone path leading to the dark mass of the sea wall. His hand trembles.

–I didn't know how to get back.

His hand drops. He forgets, he sees her, he forgets. He says to the traveler:

–Did she explain to you? She needs to sleep.

He says to the traveler:

–You have to cross the river, it's after the station, between the two branches of the river.

–What?

–S. Thala prison, the administration.

They stand up, go out.

•

Night.

In the electric light the traveler is writing.

The traveler pushes the letter away, sits there.

In front of him, the empty road, across the road, dark villas, their gardens. Beyond the gardens, the depths, elusive, S. Thala, looming.

He takes up the letter again. He writes.

S. Thala 14 September.

Don't come now, don't come, tell the children something, it doesn't matter what.

The hand stops, starts again:

If you can't figure out how to explain it to them, let them make something up.

He puts down the pen, picks it up again:

Regret nothing, nothing, silence all pain, all comprehension, tell yourself that this way you will be as close as possible to –his hand pauses, starts again, writes: *understanding.*

The traveler pushes the letter away.

He leaves the room.

The room lit up, with no one inside.

•

Night. S. Thala. Deserted.

He walks. The traveler, the man from the hotel.

He crosses the river, walks alongside the train station.

The sea rises between silt embankments. The sky stirs, overcast, dark, black in places. The station is closed.

He turns. It is there. The river forks. It is there, between the branches of the river.

It is a large stone building, simple. The steps lead to an area bordered by the branches of the river.

She is there, sleeping on the top step, leaning against the wall of the building, in the same pose as at the beach.

He is there as well. He is standing at the far end of the island, facing the mouths of the rivers, where they open to the sea.

He is speaking.

The traveler crosses onto the island. There are traces of the storm, broken branches. He walks in front of her, comes nearer, sees that she is sleeping soundly. Her breathing is regular, easy.

The traveler continues toward the tip of the island, about twenty meters from the sleeping woman.

But he stops halfway.

He sits down on a bench, halfway between the sleeping woman and the man speaking at the tip of the island.

From the outer banks of the river, from every direction, boats are moving out to sea. You can see them, passing the mouths of the river in a long chain.

Suddenly, a moan.

Suddenly, between the sound of the motors and the sound of the sea, rises a child's moan. It seems to come from the spot where she is sleeping.

For a moment his voice persists, this solitary voice swirls across the island, blends with the moaning, seeps between the noise of the motors and the roar of the sea.

Then it stops.

He must have heard the moaning.

He leaves the tip of the island. He comes back. He sees the other one, the traveler, he stops close to the bench.

–Ah, you came.

He walks away, moving toward the steps. He leans over her, he listens, he stands back up, he comes back, still hurried. He walks back to the bench, stops, announces:

–She is sleeping well.

The moaning continues.

–This moaning, it's coming from her?
–Yes, she is getting impatient, you see, but she sleeps—he pauses—it's just anger, it's nothing.
–At what?

He gestures vaguely around himself.

–At God—he continues—at God in general, it's nothing.

He walks away briskly, goes back to the tip of the island.

The noise grows louder. And the moaning. And the churning mouths of the river.

The traveler joins him at the tip of the island.

He sees him clearly in the light of the sea: the way he did the first time he saw him.

The sounds of the motors grow louder, the boats move faster, the sea churns.

He speaks, he says:

> –What a mess.—he adds—we should wait another hour, there won't be any more launchings and I think the sea will have stopped rising—it's getting late.

He points to the swirling mouth of the river:

> –Look, look. Here, look.

He points to the swollen river, the roiling water, the combining forces of the water, the brutal rising of salt toward her slumber.

A moaning. A moan, crying out:

The traveler says:

> –It's hard returning to the hotel, I don't like leaving her . . .

He responds, conflicted:

> –I understand . . . He points ahead—I understand . . . As for me, I can't . . . stand to look . . .

He points to everything around him.

Again the moaning.

It appears the one looking at the sea does not hear it anymore.

The traveler leaves the tip of the island, he comes back toward the sleeping woman. He sits down beside her limp body, looks at her. Her lips are parted. The dreaming animal groan becomes softer. She is completely asleep. He leans over, places his ear on her chest, hears the moan of a child in time with the beat of her heart, a child's moan, an angry heart.

He stands up. He fights off dizziness.

He walks, stops, starts again. He crosses once more the length of the island, going one more time toward the one watching the movement of the waters.

The sea continues to rise. The river swells. The embankments are flooding. The sea inches closer and closer to ground level.

He signals to the traveler to come closer, to look.

He says, gesturing:

–Look, look over there.

Fog arrives, very thin, from the mouths of the river. It dances before their eyes, it settles, the sea tears it to shreds, but other strands of fog arrive, dancing. He says:

–Look—he smiles.

Throughout, the angry moan of the child.

Already the movement of the river's mouths is harder to make out. The devouring salt subsides.

The traveler points to the front steps. He asks:

–Tell me a little bit about it.

He does not turn around, sees only in front of him, answers:

–I think, the island emerged first—he points to
the sea—from there. S. Thala came after, with the
dust—he adds—you know? Time . . .

As the time between the boats' departures grows, silence. He
says:

–When the moments grow longer, silence begins.

The moans become less frequent.

–Look.

A valley of water begins to form between the silt embankments.
At the mouths, a difference is now discernable: the sea fringed with
white, the salt separates, no longer penetrates. The ridges of waves
flatten.
The anger, the moaning, cease.
A final stream of words flows out of him. His eyes sparkle and
close in the peace of the waters.

–The object of absolute desire—he says—night-
slumber, around this time in general, no matter
where she is, open to the four winds—he pauses,
continues—object of desire, she belongs to whoever
wants her, she carries it and sends it along, the object
of absolute desire.

His eyes open. He turns toward this other man, the traveler,
then toward the sleeping woman, his gaze floats across S. Thala,
then drifts away.

They walk toward the sleeping body.

They come closer, look at it. The sky becomes perfectly clear.

They are seated beside the sleeping body. Her lips have closed again. The breathing, patiently, makes a path to the breathing of everyone together.

He looks at her the way he was looking at the sea a moment before, with a violent passion. The traveler asks:

–When did it begin?

He turns toward him, stares blankly; he is suddenly flooded with certainty:

–I think it was in the light, the burst of light.

He continues to look at him, recognizes him, in the transparency of his eyes everything drowns out, comes together, he says:

–You came to S. Thala for her, that's why you
came to S. Thala.

He points to her. She looks at them: she is sleeping with her eyes open.

The traveler leaves the island. He follows.

They walk.

They walk alongside the station. He shows the traveler the depths, the expanse of S. Thala.

–Her children are in there, that thing, she has
them, she gives them away—he adds—the town, the
land, is full of them.

He stops, points into the distance, in the direction of the sea, of the sea wall:

> –She has them there, where the scream came from, she leaves them, they come and take them away.

He stares in the direction of the sea wall, continues:

> –This is a realm of sands.

The traveler repeats:

> –Of sands.
> –Of wind.

He turns toward the traveler.
They look at each other:

> –Do you remember at all? The day of the scream . . . do you remember?
> –Little. Very little.

Again he shows the traveler the unbroken chain of lights:

> –She's lived everywhere, here and there. A hospital, a hotel, fields, parks, roads—he pauses—a casino, did you know that? Now she's there.

He points to the island. The traveler asks:

–A prison beyond the walls?
–That's it.
–Within the walls there is crime?

He responds distractedly:

–Crime, et cetera.

They are still walking. The traveler pronounces certain words.

–Outside, voluntary imprisonment.

He doesn't hear, he is looking toward the sea, toward the horizon, a light in the sky, he says:

–The moon, look, the lunatic moon.

They walk on, slowly. The traveler asks:

–Has she forgotten?
–Nothing.
–Gone?
–Burned. But it's all there, scattered.

He gestures carelessly toward the unbroken chain, the dark mass.
He stops, looks once more at the sea, for a long time, then he returns to the island, to her side.

•

Night.

The traveler walks along the edge of the sea.

He walks alongside the hotel behind the wall, passes it.

He walks on a road, makes his way toward a house on a hill.

He stops in front of the house. All around the house, the mass, the dizzying vista of S. Thala.

The house is gray, rectangular, with white shutters. It overlooks the beach, the mass of the sea wall, the poisoned city. The garden neglected, grass very tall, higher than the walls.

The half-open gate beckons, frightens.

The traveler walks away.

He walks back down the road, heads down toward the beach. He does not go toward the sea wall, he goes instead toward the wall that separates the sea from the city.

The traveler enters the ballroom of the hotel beyond the wall. The spot is dimly lit. Two rows of armchairs, facing the sea. A door opens onto a balcony. Dark plants rustle in the wind blowing through the open door. Parallel mirrors cover the walls. They reflect the pillars in the center of the hall, their massive shadows multiplied, the green plants, white walls, pillars, plants, pillars, walls, pillars, walls, the walls, and then, him, the traveler, who has just walked by.

•

Daylight.

She is in the courtyard of the hotel when the traveler comes out. She is wearing the clothes she was wearing that night. She is waiting for him, eyes fixed on the white façade. Standing straight, in the open air, looking at the hotel.

She hears his footsteps, sees him, comes toward him.

–I came.

–I was coming to find you—he adds—Did you know I would come?

She does not understand.

–Where?
–To the island. Did you know?
–No.

She comes closer to him, puts her head on his shoulder in a gesture of bewilderment, of fear. She looks cold. She says:

–I know this place.

She raises her head, looks at the hotel, looks at him, adds:

–I knew you once.

He remains silent. Bewilderment growing, she looks again at the hotel.

–I came to the island last night.
–Oh.
–And I met you on the beach.

Head raised, she looks at the plain white façade of the building rising up against the sea, he has trouble getting her to follow him.

He takes her with him, they walk away from the hotel.

The beach.

There are a few people strolling in the distance, horses moving slowly along. The sky is calm, the air clear.

They walk toward the sea, on the bare sand.

She is still cold, the hotel haunts her, she turns back toward the hotel. He turns her back around, leads her on. She says:

> –I asked him where you lived, he asked me to tell him what you were like, I told him—she pauses—so he told me how to find you—she looks searchingly at him—I wasn't wrong, was I?
> –No, it's all right.

She trembles again. Once more, the hotel behind them. He draws her attention to it. He points at it:

> –Had you already seen it?
> –No—she adds—I never go that way, on that side of S. Thala.

He leads her farther. She follows.

She sees the sea. She says:

> –Sometimes it's calm here.

She seems to begin to forget the hotel.

> –Not a sound.

She points to it, the morning sea, it pulses, green, cool, she moves forward, smiles, says:

–The sea.

She stops again. He keeps walking. She starts looking behind
her again.

–Come on.
–I have to go.

She only ever follows the other man from S. Thala, she must be
afraid to follow the traveler.
He sits down, calls her.

–Come, sit. We'll stop here.

She comes. She sits close to him. Is silent.
Then she looks for the other man on the beach.
The traveler is the one who spots him first.

–He's not far away, look.

In the distance, from behind the sea wall, he appears. He walks
in the tireless direction of the sea.
She has seen him. The color comes back to her cheeks. A slow
release. The memory of the hotel recedes.
She looks at him, the traveler. She is no longer trembling. He
has stretched out on the sand, she is still looking at him. She must
notice a bit of the fatigue on the traveler's face. She touches his
sleepless eyes. She says:

–I came to see you about this trip.

He calls her again.

–Come close to me.

She edges over to him, leans over, puts her head on his chest and rests there.

–I hear your heart.
–I'm dying.

She raises her head slightly. He is not looking at her. He repeats:

–I'm dying.

He has let out a little cry. The sentence hangs in the air. But the cry makes her sit up, draw back slightly from him. She leans over him, speechless, suddenly distrustful. She hesitates. She says:

–No.

She has spoken softly. In this softness the brutality of the cry is blunted, the vague threat disperses.
She begins again:

–I came to see you about that trip you wanted to take.

She is silent. He does not question her. The sentence hangs in the air, she does not know how it ends. It will end later, she can feel it; she does not rush things, just waits.

At the other end of the beach, along the sea wall, the walking has resumed. The pace is even. He walks away, he returns. He is visible the whole way. She points to him, slowly says:

> –He told me several names this morning when I was looking for you—she pauses—I chose that of S. Thala.

She does not move, attentive to the unfolding of her own words.

> –That's how we know one another—she adds— I've been here a long time and you must have known that—she continues—you must have known something about that.

Flowing sand, continuous. The steps of the mad man beat in time with her words.

> –So you came—she continues—you came to S. Thala for me.

She examines him from head to toe, makes a sign of denial, says "no," denies the accidental thought that has just come over her. She says to herself: no. Then she says with certainty:

> –You came here to kill yourself.

She waits. He does not respond. It is as if he were sleeping. She touches him, adds:

> –Otherwise you wouldn't have seen me.

She asks him:

–Do you understand?

He nods that he understands. She falls silent. He asks:

–Nobody has ever seen you?

She says clearly:

–Everybody sees me—she waits—but you saw
something more.

She points to the walker in the distance, she adds:

–Him.

She is stock still, facing the sea. He says:

–I had forgotten about both of you.
–Yes, that's it—she slowly scans the space—so
you came to S. Thala to kill yourself and then you
saw that we were still here.
–Yes.
–And you called yourself back?
–Yes—he adds—from– He stops.
–I don't know how to say it.

They fall silent.
A shadow passes in front of the sun. The wind rises, dies down.
The sea will soon change directions. The change is coming.

The walk, far off, continues along the shore.

She gets up, turns toward the sea wall, toward the walking:

> –I'm going to go see him, I'll be back.

He does not stop her. She stands close to him, but she still has her eyes on the one who walks in the distance.

> –I have to ask him something—she repeats—I'll come back.

She hesitates. She still has something to say to him.

> –About this trip—she stops—I don't understand how it is that I know that we're supposed to take it.

She points off in the distance:

> –He'll tell me.

She walks away, he calls her back. He asks:

> –S. Thala, that's my name.
> –Yes—she explains to him, gestures: –Everything, here, it's all S. Thala.

She walks away. He does not call her back. She walks along the edge of the sea.

He watches her walk. She walks more quickly than usual.

Suddenly she slows, matches his pace.

She has caught up with him. She begins to walk with him.

Instead of retracing his steps, he continues, she walks with him.

The tide has changed. The ebb of the river is underway, gliding into the abyss of salt. In bursts of white, seagulls. Near the bare sand. Their cries of hunger precede them.

The two are no longer anywhere to be seen.

They reappear a long time after.

He comes back along the edge of the water. She takes the boardwalk: she sees nothing, she avoids looking at the white swarms, the vast expanse.

They head toward the river.

The traveler does not go to the island that night.

·

It is the beginning of the afternoon. They pass by.

He, along the edge of the sea. She, on the boardwalk.

The traveler is on the boardwalk.

She does not see him. She does not see anything.

They walk toward the sea wall. Disappear behind it.

Perhaps they are preparing for the birth of the child, over there, behind the wall of the cry of S. Thala.

They come back that night. The seagulls screech. She walks bent slightly forward, almost heavily: its seems as if the birth of the child is imminent.

Doesn't call them.

·

The traveler waits elsewhere, waits for them in the hotel ballroom. He is waiting for them at a different time. At night. At night, in the great hall.

The room has changed appearance. The mirrors are tarnished. The armchairs are facing the mirrors, lined up along the white walls. Only the dark plants are still in place. They are still rustling in the wind coming through the open door. Slow movements of the pernicious swell of the sea, of dead spirits.

He arrives in the dark of night. She has not come, he is alone. He enters the room quickly, he sees the traveler seated in an armchair against the wall. He says:

−I was passing by.

He adds:

−I never come this way.

He sits down, looks around.
Suddenly he sees the room.
All around him, the room.
He looks at it.
His eyes sparkle. It is almost completely dark. He looks around as if it were broad daylight. For a long time.
He moves.
He goes toward the balcony, turns, looks around again intently. Comes back. Walks back in front of the traveler seated in the shadowy half-light, does not see him anymore, sees only the room.
Suddenly, he stops in the middle of the dance floor, with a wave of his hand he traces the space between the rows of armchairs and the pillars, asks:

−Was it here?—he stops—Over there?

His voice wavers.

He waits.

Standing in the middle of the dance floor, he is still waiting.

Then, once again, he points to the space, traces the space between the lined up armchairs, he repeats the gesture, waits, says nothing.

Walks, up and down the space, walks across it again, stops.

Walks. Stops again. Freezes.

Someone is singing, very low.

Someone is singing.

He is singing.

It is the music of the long dead parties of S. Thala, the heavy strains of its step.

He walks forward. All of a sudden his usual stiffness disappears. Here he is, walking forward, singing and dancing at the same time, moving out onto the dance floor, dancing, singing.

He is swept away, remembers, dances to the sway of the music, is consumed, burns, he is mad with happiness, he dances, burns, a burning pierces the night of S. Thala.

A few seconds. He stops.

He is still. He is no longer moving. No longer singing, he tries to understand what has happened, what has interrupted the dancing, the song. He is seized by dizziness.

Movement at the back of the hall.

He asks:

–Who's there?

He listens to his own voice. The steadiness of his gaze is unwavering. He is subject to his own words the way, a few minutes earlier, he was to his own movement.

He repeats:

–Who's there?

He seems afraid, turns, stands up taller.

The traveler has risen. He walks slowly from the back of the room.

He looks at this other man, the traveler. This man, the traveler, takes a few steps, steps into the light of the dance floor. He looks at him.

He sees him.

The stillness shatters, his mouth opens, no sound escapes, he tries again to speak, fails, falls back into an armchair, extends his hand to the traveler, looks at him as he did the first time he saw him, murmurs:

–You, it was you—he pauses—you have returned.

He weeps.

•

Sunday. The sound has not grown in S. Thala. Some wind. Then rain.

The traveler is walking in S. Thala in the rain.

He does not encounter them.

A night. A day.

The traveler does not see them anywhere in the space, the time of S. Thala.

•

A dark night.

She walks by, in front of the hotel.

The traveler is on the balcony, he sees her go by on the board-walk, her shadow stands out against the sea.

She is walking slowly, steadily toward the sea wall. She does not turn back to the hotel. She walks, in the night, straight ahead.

The child, it is the child, its birth.

He, the other man, follows her tonight. She moves forward, unaware. He follows. She forges ahead, bestial, she walks.

She disappears behind the dark mass of the sea wall, she vanishes into the sands, the boundless wind.

Then he vanishes. Disappears.

Nothing left. But the vast, dormant depths.

•

The next day, sunny.

The traveler skirts S. Thala in the sun.

He walks off, does not enter. He walks along a road lined with shuttered houses: islands in an ocean of stone.

He is searching in S. Thala, beyond it.

•

Sunshine still.

The traveler walks in front of an occupied house. There is a terrace on the grounds. You can catch a glimpse from the road. The windows are open. Someone is speaking inside the house.

A woman laughs—a quick, delicate laugh.

Broad daylight.

The traveler retraces his steps.

He moves off.

•

Evening, on the banks of the river, on the island. She is alone, seated on the bank, looking straight ahead of her, at S. Thala. The traveler sits down beside her, she sees him:

–Ah, you came.

She is completely absorbed by what she sees. He asks her:

–Did you ask him about the trip?

She remembers:

–He says that I always talked about this trip whenever I was in S. Thala.

The sun is setting. She is about to fall asleep from the effort of looking at S. Thala. She must already be waiting for the other man to escort her off to sleep.

Her face shows no sign of fatigue or pain. But she has lost weight and there is a smiling strength in her eyes.

She notices that the traveler is walking away.

•

The traveler walks back in front of the occupied house. He stops. From the street, you can see the terrace, a part of the garden.

He rings the doorbell. The door opens automatically from the inside, he enters. The place is very bright, furnished in white.

A woman's voice:

–What is it?

He does not answer, cannot. Before him a glass door is open onto the terrace. The voice is coming from the part of the terrace he cannot see. He waits.

She appears, backlit, in the glass. She is wearing a summer dress. She has black hair, tousled.

She can barely see him in the half-light of the doorway.

–Well, who are you looking for?

He steps forward, says nothing. She can still barely see him.

–Well, what do you want?

He takes another step toward her. She watches him approach, she smiles, is surprised, but seems to feel no fear.

He takes one more step, he stops. He has stepped into the light of the terrace.

She sees him.

She looks away suddenly. Her face freezes, her eyes, an uncontrollable shudder travels through her body.

She goes toward the terrace, he follows her. She makes a mechanical gesture, she points to an armchair, she says:

–Sit down, please.

They are standing, motionless. She murmurs:

–You've come back . . .

They do not look at each other.
He remains standing beside her. She does not sit down. She leans against the table on the terrace.
She takes out a cigarette. Her hand is trembling.
She sits down.
She is seated in the shade of a blue umbrella.
He begins to look at her: the beauty is there, still present.
There is a coffee table to her right, on top of it there is an open book. There is a path in front of her. At the end, a white gate, closed. The grounds extend in green lawns all the way up to it.

–She never got better?
–Never.

She turns away, toward the garden, her head falling against the back of the armchair, she says:

–Sometimes . . . I think she's calling me . . . still
. . . even now . . .

She struggles. Her jaw clenches to hold back tears.
She is not crying for herself.
He is still looking at her, intently. She does not notice.

–I knew full well she wasn't dead, somebody would have told me—she hesitates and asks, in a lower voice—Where did she end up?
–In S. Thala prison.
–Ah . . .

She puts the image out of her mind, leaning back in her chair.
Her body is visible under her dress. Her body is still alive. Her
legs are bare, her feet are bare against the stone of the terrace.

The traveler is still looking at her with the same unnatural
attention. She still does not notice. She murmurs again, asks:

–Does she still speak of me?
–No.

She takes out another cigarette. She is still trembling. Her eyes
are very dark, lined with black makeup, bottomless pits into which
sense is lost.

She stares absently at a point on the ground.

–I suppose there is nothing anyone can do for
her, is there?
–Nothing.

She is still completely unaware of the unfathomable attention of
which she is the object. She asks:

–Why did you come back to S. Thala?

Silence. She is surprised.
She turns toward him. Meets his gaze.
He tries to respond. He begins to respond:

–I'm not sure I wanted to—he stops.

He shakes his head, he searches again for a way to respond:

–No . . . that's not true . . . no . . . —he adds—I
wanted to.
  –What?
  –Kill myself—he adds—I was looking for a place
to do it, I ran into her.

She sits up slightly in her chair—in an instant her eyes focus on
the grounds and she sees once more everything that has happened—
then her eyes move back and she says:

  –That's it . . . that's it indeed . . . No matter
where she goes, everything falls to pieces.

The traveler does not notice the error in the chronology of
death.

  –Death becomes pointless?
  –Yes.

Now she looks at him. They look at each other. He says:

  –I'm not sure I recognize you.

Change happens with the same brutality of day passing to night:

  –How have I changed?

He shrugs: he is not sure what has changed.
  She starts to smile. She smiles. Her face changes imperceptibly.
She smiles.

–You don't see?

The smile is frozen in the middle of her face. Beneath it, the face becomes hardly recognizable. She continues to smile.
She is no longer recognizable. She says:

–Look at me.

She gets up. She stands in front of him, upright, rigid. Her whole body in front of him, her face, her smile.

–You don't think so?
–No.

She sits back down.

–Look again.

She leans forward: it is around the face. He says:

–Your hair.
–Yes—the smile grows.
–Dyed.
–Yes. Black—she adds, the smile growing even wider—my black hair dyed black—she continues—Is that all?

A mounting dread, terrace, grounds, places of terror all of a sudden. The traveler rises, he leans on the table, no longer looks at her. She continues looking at him, still waiting for the response, she smiles:

–So? You don't see?—she points around her at the house, the grounds, the enclosed space within the walls, the railings, the fences—You don't see anything?

He shakes his head: nothing, he no longer sees anything. She says:

–The dead woman of S. Thala.

She repeats:

–I am the dead woman of S. Thala.

She waits, then finishes:

–I made it through.

She waits once more, finishes:

–The only one of all of you—she adds—the only one, the dead woman of S. Thala.

She turns toward her garden, her house. She no longer finishes any sentence. The smile is still there, nothing left beneath it but lines.

He leaves. She lets him go. She stays there. There.

He takes the path, opens the gate, goes out.

Outside. Space. Seagulls flying by.

•

Black smoke above S. Thala.

Broad daylight.

The traveler looks out the window of his room.

The clamor of fire alarms, coming from the river.

The traveler looks at his watch, then once again at the black smoky sun.

The sirens stop.

You can hear footsteps outside.

A woman crosses the courtyard, she goes toward the great hall. She is accompanied by two children. They are in mourning clothes.

The traveler steps back from the window, waits, listens, waits.

The alarms start up again, sounding across the whole city, furiously raging.

The smoke continues to rise above S. Thala from the direction of the river.

In S. Thala, a thick unmoving heat. The shade of the trees glued to the ground of S. Thala. The wind has deserted it. A sun fastened to an empty sky caps it.

The traveler goes toward the table, takes the letter, puts it in an envelope and places it back on the table.

He leaves his room.

The hallway: at the end, the man who walks.

He is in the light from the windows in the stairwell.

He is waiting.

They look at each other. The mouth laughs, blue eyes flash in the burned face.

He points in the direction of the sirens, announces:

–Fire.

His eyes have a liquid transparency. He adds:

–The prison—he adds—it was put out when I left—he stops, informs him—It burns often.

The sirens wail. The traveler says:

–It's still burning.
–Yes, but farther away—he stops—it's always burning somewhere.

The sirens have stopped. The traveler asks:

–You were passing through?
–I'm looking for her—he explains—Sometimes she goes past the limits of S. Thala and you just have to know that.

He looks around, he adds:

–Unless she's here.
–No.

He walks away, remembers something, comes back.

–Somebody is asking for you in the lobby, I told them to wait.

He leaves.
The traveler stays where he is, waits.
For a long time. Then someone arrives.
Someone comes up the stairs. He recognizes her. The woman who crossed the courtyard. She sees him at the top of the stairs.

The sirens have ceased. She looks at him, she says:

–Somebody told me you were here, a man I didn't know.

She continues up the stairs. He does not look at her. She comes closer.

–We can go to your room—her tone is timid, frightened.

He looks at the windows of the hallway. She says:

–I hardly recognize you.

She touches his shoulder, repeats:

–Can we go to your room to talk?

He says—his voice is slow, soft, broken all of a sudden:

–I wrote to you. The letter is still there.

•

She puts the letter back on the table. She is standing. He looks out the window at the motionless city, smoke above the island.

The sirens sweep past, across the city. She says—her voice is low, hushed:

–I don't really understand . . .

He looks at her: his gaze vacant. She draws back. She is trembling.

–You stopped . . .

He tries to respond, cannot. She continues:

–I even ask myself if . . . if even in the beginning
. . . you ever—she stops.

He says:

–Probably not.

The sirens again, wailing, deafening, across S. Thala. She stops
speaking, afraid, she cries out:

–What is that?
–Fire.

She screams with the sirens:

–Where is it?
–Far.

He listens to the sirens, trying to discern which direction they
race toward. His distraction unleashes her anger, she shouts again:

–There's something else, I'm sure of it, there's
something else.

The sirens fade and fade, taper off in the distance.

He looks straight ahead, the empty street, the never-ending sun.
Her anger yields.
Suddenly she begs:

–Talk to me, I beg you.

He says:

–I want to see the children again.

He closes his eyes, takes a step. She thinks he is going to leave, she holds him back.

–Don't leave before I know . . .

He says:

–I want to see the children.

He waits.
She does not reply. She looks at him for a long time, draws nearer, hesitates, draws nearer still:

–How long has it been going on?

His tone is calm, flat. He says:

–Forever.

She lets out an exclamation, a brief, forced laugh. He watches: her face is frozen in silent laughter, her eyes beg him:

—Are you making fun of me?
—No.

The sincerity of his response is frightening. She draws back. When she draws back he realizes his mistake. He moves toward her, makes a sign of apology, says:

—Understand me—he stops, adds—I wanted to say . . . I've only known it for a few days.

She waits: nothing, he says nothing more. She says:

—You're hurting me . . .

He does not reply.
She cries out again, but weakly, her anger quelled.

—I'd like an explanation . . . It seems to me I have a right to one . . .

He has not heard.

—What have I done wrong?
—Nothing . . . I . . .

He is in front of her. She sees him struggle to speak, sees his inability to do so. She takes his hand. He lets her. Finally he says:

—Something is happening, something uncon-scious—he adds—something essential.

She lets go of his hand, gasps:

> −Are you doing this on purpose?
> −No.

She waits: nothing else, he says nothing else.

He has forgotten her presence, he is watching the street. Abruptly, with sudden understanding, she sees the futility of reasoning.

> −Well then . . . Is it serious?

In a stupefied tone:

> −You mean that . . .
> −Yes.

She hesitates one last time:

> −And she wants you?
> −Yes.

She pauses. He says nothing. Waits some more, a long time, nothing.

Then she moves. She walks.

She paces about the room, up and down. Sounds of stifled sobs. And, barely audible:

> −And me, poor me, who didn't suspect a thing . . .

All of a sudden she stops.

Stands still.

She has stopped beside the bedside table. She holds in her hand a small glass bottle full of white pills, unopened. She looks at it, reads the label on the bottle.

The sirens sweep by, a whirlwind on the road in front of the hotel, still heading in the direction of the river.

She puts down the bottle. For a long time she looks at the man in front of her. She passes her hand across her face to ward off the vision.

He sees her. He makes a gesture of apology, but does not manage to say anything.

She asks in the same stupefied tone:

–What does it mean . . . ?

He motions: nothing, he motions that it is nothing.

She silently moves closer to him, she moves in very close to his face, close enough to touch it, says:

–I know you, you won't do it.

The sirens, again, from the direction of the river.
They stop.
She says calmly:

–The children are in the great hall.

Sirens, again, from the river.

•

The children.

They rise, watch him approach. They are pale in their black clothes. They are motionless, watching him, only him.

They are side by side, standing a meter apart, in the same expectant pose. They have been told of the tragedy, they are unaware of its nature.

He stops. He looks at them.

He looks at each in turn, the one, then the other. He sees them singly, then together. He does not come closer.

He is separated from them by a rectangle of sunlight created by the balcony doors. No one steps into the rectangle of light. There is no fear in the eyes of the children. Only an anxiety.

Their mother is somewhere in the hall, they do not see her.

They are looking at this man who is silent. They wait.

He says:

–I'm never coming back.

The news is received with silence.

The look on the children's faces has not changed.

The anxiety remains the same.

–Never?

The voice is neutral, mechanical.

–Never.

The adult voice is as calm as that of the child.

The woman crosses the rectangle of light separating the man from the children, she needs air, she runs toward the balcony, bumps into the door, stops there, against the door, hiding her face in her hands.

The children do not see her. They see the man and only him.

–Why?

The voice is clear, still calm, completely colorless.

–I don't want children anymore.

The anxiety is the same, it is boundless. Their mouths are open in boundless need to understand. No sign of suffering. The other child's voice:

–Why?
–I don't want anything anymore.

The woman moves, she walks through the door, comes back in from the balcony. She has let out a muted cry of suffocation.

The tension in the faces has remained the same. So has the anxiety.

The wail of sirens breaks out all over the city.

The woman runs in, cries out.

–What is that? Is it here?

Neither the man, nor the children reply.

The sirens suddenly die down. They stop.

Still in the same lucid voice, one of the children connects a series of events that are, on the face of it, unrelated:

–The police came when you were upstairs.

The other child raises an arm and points in the direction of the river while still looking at the man:

–There's a fire, it was because of the fire.

An isolated cry: the mother. She shouts that they must leave.

–Let's get out of here.

The children speak calmly as the sirens wail and the woman screams:

–They were looking for somebody who was with you.
–A woman who escaped, they were afraid.

The woman screams:

–We have to get out of here, I can't take it any more.

The children do not hear her.
She rushes toward them:

–Come on, we're leaving.

She rushes over, she shoves them along. The little boy stumbles. She takes his hand, stands him up, pushes him, grabs the little girl, shoves her as well, pushes her, pushes them in front of her, cannot quite gather them, pushes, moves them forward, wails, wails with the sirens:

—Get moving or I'll start screaming again.

They will not budge, they are still looking at him, glued to the spot.

She is afraid, cries out:

—I'm scared, come on.

Their need remains as insatiable as at the first moment. They are still waiting. The anxiety will go unanswered.

She pushes them, pushes them forward, forward, pushes, pushes with all her strength toward the door of the hall.

The door.

She has reached it.

The door, again. It bangs shut. Someone is walking in the courtyard of the hotel.

Beyond the door of the balcony, the sand, the sea. A long time. Then he goes out.

She is against the wall, in the heat. Her eyes are almost closed. Tears stream down her face. She does not notice the traveler's presence.

It is only when he sits down beside her that she sees him.

He is silent. She says:

—Ah, you came back.

The sea is distant through her half-open eyes. The city, over there, is invisible, mired in its own excretions. There are no birds. Tears flow from her eyes. She says:

–A woman came with children.

He nods: yes. She sees him through her tears. He seems to be cold in the motionless heat. He looks down, the sand.

–They've left.
–Yes.

In the distance, above the sea, patches of shadow. The sky is clouding over. Then it rains under the patches of darkness. She watches. She weeps.

–Now you don't have anything left, either.

He does not respond.
She weeps.
Steadily, smoothly, the tears flow from her eyes.
A patch of light forms on the sea.
They do not see it.
He looks at the sand close to him: her hand lying on the sand is dirty, darkened. He says:

–Your hands are black.

She lifts her hands, looks at them, drops them.

–It's the fire.

–They were looking for you.

He takes some sand.
Touches the sand.
A patch of white light forming on the sea.
She reaches out her hand:

–The light, there.

He does not hear her. He asks:

–What are you crying about?
–All of it.

He sees that the sand, below his eyes, is getting brighter. He
raises his head, notices the light on the sea.
Turns back to the sand.

–Are you crying about the fire?
–No, about all of it.

He still does not move, does not look, does not see. On the sea,
the patch of light now formed. She points it out to him:

–There's the light, over there.

Remains riveted to the sand.
She points to the bare sky above the light.
He repeats:

–The police are looking for you.

Sirens in the distance.

> –Yes.
> –They're going to kill you.
> –I can't die.
> –That's true.

Then she points to the beach. Then to a certain spot on the beach, under the light, close to the pillars of the bombed-out casino:

> –In that same spot the other day there was a dead dog—she turns toward him—the sea swept it away during the storm.

She stops pointing, turns away from everything, retreats into the memory of the dead dog.

She stays there for a long time, the time it takes for the light to dim, to disappear. He says:

> –I saw the dead dog.
> –I thought you had seen it, too.

The patch of rainy light has disappeared.

More storms erupt.

Curtains of sun-lit rain, scattered above the sea.

He begins to watch the curtains of rain.

Rain. It won't reach S. Thala today. Only its smell makes it here: the smell of fire, of wind.

She is no longer crying. She says, she repeats:

–We can leave now—she adds—You don't have
anything left, either.

–We can—he adds—Nothing left.

·

She is no longer against the wall. Has gone toward the river.

Night. It has happened.

Some people on the boardwalk. They walk very slowly. They
speak in hushed tones of the cries they hear these days in S. Thala,
the growing fires.

The traveler rises.

He walks.

His gait is very slow, heavy.

He walks along. He turns. He walks along the beach. Then by
the closed train station. The river. After the river, he turns. The
sea is high. The boats have left S. Thala. Forsaken Babylon, far off.

On the island there are traces of fire, of burned wood, blackened
stone.

They are on the top step of the stone stairs, the place she usually
sits. They sleep intertwined. Their slumber is deep.

He sits at their side. Then falls asleep.

He wakes with the day, he is alone. They have already left for their
labor, their siege of the sands of S. Thala, the object of their walk.

·

Evening. Gold light.

She waits on the boardwalk, facing the hotel, turned toward S.
Thala. He comes toward her. She says:

–I came to see you about that trip.

She looks beyond the hotel and the grounds, the chain unbroken in space, the depth of time. She adds:

–The trip to S. Thala, you know.

He can barely see her face straining toward the depths.

–I haven't come back here since I was young.

The sentence remains, suspended for a moment, then she finishes:

–I forgot.

She stops looking at S. Thala. She smiles at him. He asks:

–What did he say?
–He said that the trip was necessary. She adds
–He didn't say why.

A cool breeze comes from the sea, gentle, the smell of seaweed and rain.

–Before—she says—it was a realm of sand.

He says:

–Of wind.

She repeats:

> –Of wind, yes.

She is standing on the boardwalk. She is not looking anymore.
She does not look at anything. She is standing, facing the breeze.
He says:

> –The rivers were big, the fields, beyond the
> shore?

She smiles:

> –Yes. She adds—we would come by train for
> summer vacation.

She repeats:

> –Summer.

They are silent. She watches him. He says:

> –We can go whenever you want.

She walks off along the boardwalk. The breeze continues, cool,
to cover the beach, the light fades beneath a clear sky.

·

Three days. Golden light.

Three days, during which nothing happens but the incessant gnawing sound that swells with the light, wanes with the light.

The sun hovers above S. Thala. Wind. Golden light, hovering, lashed by wind. The smell of salt and iodine together, an acrid odor unearthed from the waters.

The sea roils, strong, beneath the naked sky, the sands swell, run, cry, the seagulls fight against the wind, their flight thwarted.

The place at the wall remains empty, illuminated.

Then the wind falls, the sands settle. The sea calms, exposing the rot and decay of the unbroken chain of buildings. In the sky, above them, again, slow vessels of rain pour themselves out.

Three days.

Then she comes.

She arrives, less burdened now, on the boardwalk, comes toward the traveler who waits to accompany her on her last voyage into the depths of S. Thala.

•

S. Thala.

They walk. They walk into S. Thala. She walks straight, facing the wind, between the walls. The traveler says:

>   –Eighteen years. He pauses –That's how old you
>   were.

She lifts her eyes, looks out at the petrified landscape. She says:

>   –I don't know any more.

The road is flat, easy to walk without thinking. From time to time she pronounces the word, she says:

–S. Thala, my S. Thala.

Then she looks at the ground.

–I don't recognize it.

Slowly, while they walk, S. Thala passes by, its houses, their gardens.
The road turns.
After the bend, she hesitates, stops.
She looks. Before them the gray house, rectangular, with white shutters, lost in the dizziness of S. Thala.
The garden surrounds it, the grass, still green, wild, tangled in the gray shutters, spilling over the walls. She looks, she says:

–It was no use coming back.

She resumes walking.
She returns toward the dust, the surface of the roads of S. Thala, she says while walking:

–This is a different place.

They continue on.
The gardens are less grand, the houses touch each other, the walls.
They walk.

The traveler begins to look at the ground, the white ashes. He says:

> –Everything was taken away with your personal belongings.
> –When? –she slows down.
> –The first time you fell ill. He pauses –After the ball.

She does not say anything at first. She smiles:

> –Yes, I think so.

They walk. Her gaze returns to the ground. She is in white, her hair combed. He got her ready, on the island this morning, he washed her, did her hair. She carries a small girl's bag, also white, the white bag from the trip to S. Thala. She takes it and opens it. She takes out a mirror. She stops, looks at herself, starts again. She holds the mirror out to him, shows it to him.

> –He gave this to me before he left.

She opens the bag again. She puts the mirror back inside. He looks: the bag is empty, there is nothing in it but the mirror. She closes it, she says:

> –A ball.
> –Yes. He hesitates –You were, at that moment, supposed to have been in love.

She turns, smiles at him.

–Yes. After . . . she returns to the present, to the contemplation of the ground—Afterward I was married to a musician, I had two children—she stops. They took them also.

She turns toward him, explains to him:

    –You know, it was after I got sick the second time.
    –Someone told you this?
    –I remembered the children. She adds—and him.

He stops. She stops too. He has trouble speaking. She does not notice.

    –Where is he now?

In the same matter-of-fact tone, she says:

    –Dead, he's dead.

The wind from the sea begins to blow through S. Thala. He does not move anymore, he stays there, in the wind. She stands next to him, unaware of his dizziness. She is happy in the wind. She says:

    –The wind of S. Thala, it's the same.

He looks at her.
Stopped in front of her, he looks at her.

She must see something of the violence in his eyes. She looks for the object of this violence, amazed, she asks:

–What is it?
–I'm looking at you.

She asks:

–There is no trip, is there?
–No. We are in S. Thala, trapped. He adds –I'm looking at you.

She walks, docile, toward him. He clasps her against his body. She lets him. He releases her. She lets him release her.
They resume walking.
The yards have disappeared, the gardens.
The road rises.
The sea ebbs, the sands grow. She turns, looks.
He recites:

–"Rows of poplars fell down behind the train. He watched her."

She laughs, walks.
He recites:

–"Plains, fields, the spindly walls of white trees. He watched her."

She laughs again, walks on.
They continue on.

A change occurs. The road widens. A town square. The wind from the sea ceases little by little.

She looks around again.

They stop. The change becomes more noticeable. No more wind. The sun intensifies.

Heat rises from the stones.

Barely surprised, she smiles in the bright glare of her hometown, she says:

–So it's summer in S. Thala?

They begin to walk again.

They cross the empty square.

She slows down, already the fatigue begins.

The heat intensifies.

The sun swells.

They have crossed the square. As soon as they leave it, here they are, here they are all of a sudden, appearing from everywhere, from the holes, from the stone, completely indifferent to one another, bustling with activity, the residents of S. Thala.

They follow them.

With equal attention she watches the residents of S. Thala, their homes, the man who is next to her and the sea in the distance, here—on the front of a building they are walking past—combined with the words "GOVERNMENT OF," the name of S. Thala, and over there, very far off, the white bursts of seagulls and the sands, distinct.

She, too, suffers from the heat, the inexplicable onslaught of light.

They follow them still.

She slows down more and more.

They pass the people, leave them behind.

She stops:

a long, straight boulevard.

Suddenly, once they have made their way through the bustle and activity of the square, they find themselves on this boulevard, long and straight.

She does not move.

Suddenly contemptuous, she begins to look suspiciously at the stretch of boulevard before her.

The sun burns. Her eyes seem to sting, she looks ahead as if forced to do so.

She starts walking again.

Again she looks vacantly ahead, seeing nothing.

They start walking.

The road is long, straight. You cannot see the end.

She walks with squinted eyes, to avoid suffering the onslaught of light. She does not speak to him. She walks.

All around, the white walls, the unfolding of S. Thala. Treeless road.

Nobody but the traveler has seen him: before them, at the end of the boulevard, in his dark clothes, walking swiftly. They have been following him without knowing it ever since they left the sands of S. Thala.

The bright walls pulse, they multiply on either side of the walk.

She must feel hot, she wipes her face with her hand, she slows down, she starts again. They advance very slowly.

The walls increase in number, they multiply, intersect, come one after the other, come together, they beat on the temples, make the eyes bleed. Still no shade.

Still ahead of them, the black silhouette against the whiteness of the walls at the end of the boulevard.

She still does not see him.

She walks forward.

She stops.

It is she who stops. Her eyes on the ground, suddenly, she knows: the distance between the heart of S. Thala and the sea has remained counted off in the remembered paces of her childhood: she lifts her eyes, she says:

–Look at what they built.

There is a nondescript building, big, it would seem, white as chalk. Many entrances; they are closed: wooden shutters nailed shut.

–This used to be an open square.

She remains still. She repeats:

–There was a square once, and they put that in its place.

She turns and sees him, the other one, stopped as well, and waiting. She says suddenly:

–I have to sleep.

At once she starts walking. The traveler holds her back. He says:

–I remember, too.

They look: the building imposing, its form, its size. Pierced by nails.

The traveler says:

–There was a square. He corrects himself—a surface, flat, a square surrounded by walls, in the walls
there was a door.

They look at each other. They see each other.

–Perhaps . . . she murmurs.

Suddenly her eyes close, open, her gaze resurfaces. She waits, she
does not look at him anymore, looks at the ground, he does not go
on. She resumes walking.

All of a sudden she begins walking quickly.

The sea. She sees it.

Once they pass the building, there it is.

It was there, very close. The heart of S. Thala opening out onto
the sea.

The road stops: ahead, no one walking anymore.

There is a boardwalk. They cross it. Here is the beach, without
walls, the sea, the sands, the waters of the sea.

To their left the expanse of the heart of S. Thala spreads out. Its
outline looms over the beach.

She collapses on the sand, stretches out, does not move anymore.

•

The sands of S. Thala.

He sits next to her. Slowly he wipes the sweat from her forehead.
At his touch, she closes her eyes. She drops the little bag she has
been holding. She says:

–There's the noise.

He continues to stroke her forehead.

–Sleep.
–Yes.

She turns her cheek against the sand, she listens, says:

–Tonight, it comes from over there.

She points to the beach, the sand. He says:

–I hear it as well.
–Ah . . .

She asks very low:

–They're dead?
–No.
–What happened to them?
–They're resting. He adds –Or nothing.

She murmurs:

–Ah yes . . . true . . . true . . .

He lies down next to her, leans on his free hand, looks at her.
He has never looked at her from so close. He has never seen her in
such stark light. She is still listening to the sound. She closes her
eyes. She wills them closed, her eyelids trembling from the effort.

–Tell me to sleep.

He tells her:

–Sleep.
–Yes—her tone is hopeful.

She touches the sand. He says:

–We're back on the beach. Sleep.
–Yes.

He stops stroking her forehead, puts his hand over her eyes to shade them from the sun.

–Sleep.

She is silent.
He waits.
She does not move. He lifts his hand. Underneath her eyes are closed. The lids tremble in the sun, but they do not open.
She sleeps.
He picks up some sand, sprinkles it on her body. She breathes, the sand moves, trickling off her body. He takes some more, does it again. The sand trickles again. He takes some more, sprinkling it again. He stops.

–Love.

Her eyes open, they look without seeing, without recognizing anything, then close again, fade to black.

•

He is not there anymore. She is lying alone on the sand under the sun, like the carcass of the dog, rotting, her hand still buried in the sand, near the white bag.

•

The lobby of the building is empty. Murmuring voices. And further, at the end of a corridor, the music of the wild parties long past, the song of S. Thala.

Half-light.

Beyond the lobby, a long corridor.

The traveler walks down the corridor, advancing, penetrating the darkness. From the end of the hallway a man wearing a uniform approaches.

–Are you looking for something?

They are face to face. The traveler looks at him.

–Can I help you?

They are both in the shadows. The traveler stares at him with unnatural intensity.

Finally the traveler speaks:

–You've been here a long time?
–Seventeen years. He pauses –Why?

The traveler examines his face: his eyes already glassy, his hair graying at the temples. The man grows impatient.

>   –Are you looking for someone?—His tone more
>   curt—What do you want?
>   –I'm looking.

The traveler does not move, his gaze remains riveted on the other man's face. The man makes a sign of impatience. The traveler asks:

>   –How many years did you say?
>   –Seventeen years.

The traveler looks down the corridor to the end. The question arrives, brutally.

>   –The ballroom is down that way?
>   –There were several. Which one do you mean?

The traveler points to a door at the end of the corridor.

>   –That one.

The man says:

>   –There aren't any more parties.

The man must see the anguish in the eyes of the traveler. He says:

>   –I can show it to you if you want.
>   –Thank you.

—Follow me.

The man walks ahead of the traveler, he opens the door, enters, holds it open. The traveler enters.

—Here it is—you have some memories, I see.

There are mirrors, all tarnished. Armchairs are lined up facing the mirrors, along the light-colored walls. The planters are empty.

The traveler walks to the middle of the dance floor. He stops, looks around: a small stage, a closed piano, rugs rolled up along the walls. All around the dance floor, bare tables.

He hears:

—They would dance here.

He turns. The man is smiling in the shadows, he points to the dance floor and asks:

—Do you want me to turn the lights on?
—No.

Light, sunlight, filtering through the thick curtains.

The traveler walks toward the closed door. He lifts a curtain: through closed shutters, a terrace, the beach, she who sleeps.

The traveler tries to open the door. It won't open. He rattles the knob.

—Can't you see it's locked?

The man has called out, he hurries over.

–Why are you still trying to open it, you know it's locked.

The traveler releases the door handle, stays where he is.

–I don't have the keys, the man says, regaining his composure. We're not supposed to open it.

The traveler lifts the curtain once more: the terrace, the beach, her.
The traveler turns to the man and asks:

–Do you recognize her?

The man approaches, looks out.

–The sleeping woman? He points. –Her?
–Yes.

He pretends to study her.

–From this distance—he stops. –I'm sorry—he says candidly, no, I don't recognize her.

The traveler releases the curtain. The man says:

–Sorry.

The traveler approaches, he begs:

–Recognize her.

The man asks:

    −Why?

The traveler does not respond. The man asks:

    −What is her name?

The traveler responds:

    −I don't know anything anymore.

The man says a name.
The traveler listens closely. The man asks:

    −Is that it?

The traveler does not respond. He begs:

    −Say that name again.
    −Which one?
    −The one you just said. Please.

The man steps back a bit, he repeats clearly, completely, the name he just invented.

The traveler goes toward the door, holds out his arms as if to step through, then gives up, his head sagging into his hands. Sobs erupt from him.

The man looks at him, pauses for a moment, then approaches. His voice is calm:

–You should go; go and find her.

The traveler stands up straight, his arms falling to his sides.

The man lets another moment pass, then he takes the traveler by the arm and leads him to the door. He says:

–You have to leave now; I have work to do.

They go out. The man locks the door. The music has resumed at the end of the corridor.

The man accompanies the traveler to the lobby and leaves him there.

The traveler crosses the lobby, goes out.

•

She is lying in the sun, as before. Her eyes are open. She watches the traveler approach. Her gaze is gentle, like her voice.

–You came back.

There, at the edge of the shore, the other one again, still walking. There is no living thing but him in all the empty space. The traveler says:

–I went for a walk while you were sleeping.
–Ah, she stares. I thought you'd gone.

She gestures toward the one who is walking over there, on the empty beach, in the infernal sun.

–I would have left with him. –Or the police would have taken me away.

He sits near her. She says suddenly, touching his arm, wanting him to look at her.

–Where were you? She asks—You went for a walk where?
–You were sleeping. I wanted to let you sleep.
–No.

He walks away, he comes back, over there, on the empty sands, with his regular gait, in his inscrutable state of expectation. He watches him, only him. She says:

–You went to cry. You went to ask.

Her gaze cuts through him, sharp, unrelenting. The traveler is still looking off at the tranquil walk.

–I was looking for the square between the walls.

She takes a long time to respond.

–Did you find it? Her voice is low.
–Yes. And the door we left through—he adds: Separately.

They are silent.
For a long time they watch the movement over by the water's edge.

The movement of the one who walks changes, instead of retracing his steps, he continues. She has seen him. She watches him walk away. The traveler says:

–He's watching over us.
–No, she says. Nothing.

He has turned toward the heights of the village. He disappears behind the building. The traveler, distracted, asks:

–What? What is he doing?

She turns toward him.

–Didn't I tell you?
–He's watching the sea? Watching us? Will he bring us back?
–No.

Diminishing: the heat, the sun.
She feels a little better. She sits down. Gusts of wind come and go. Behind, in the unbroken chain, the gnawing starts up again. The traveler asks:

–He watches over the movement of the tides, the light.
–No.
–The movement of the waters. The wind. The sand.
–No.
–Slumber?

–No. She hesitates. –Nothing.
The traveler is silent.

She turns toward him. She says:

–You're not talking anymore.

She remembers:

–It's true—she stops. Her voice grows tender
again. –You are nothing.

The sky darkens. The sea grows heavy, dark, muddy. Far off, the
seagulls, flesh-eaters.
She follows ahead on an unseen path.

–It's night?
–I think so.

She says suddenly, with certainty and gentleness:

–I don't know this town, S. Thala, anymore. I
never came back.

Her words resound, fade away.
They survey the beach.
Night, here it is.
He does not reappear. The traveler asks:

–He hasn't come back. Will he return?

–Yes. She adds –Sometimes he gets lost in thought but he always comes back. Tonight he will come back.

Wind blows across the water.
Night has fallen when he returns.
He does not go toward them, he goes back up toward the town of S. Thala, and this time he disappears into its depths. She repeats:

–Tonight he will return. She adds, –Tonight he must set fire to the heart of S. Thala.

•

The beach. Night.
The traveler has stretched out on the sand. She is lying near him.
They are silent. They wait.
The silence of S. Thala resounds, tonight it cries out, crackles, they listen, they follow its most secret modulations.
She says:

–Someone is talking; just over there.

Some voices in the sands. Nearby. He says:

–Lovers.

They listen to the amorous moaning, the dreadful groans of pleasure. She says:

−I can't see any more.

Far off, the first dark smoke. He says:

−I see.

The first black smoke rises in the clear sky of S. Thala.

She opens her arms in a tender gesture of desperation, she murmurs:

−S. Thala, my S. Thala.

She turns toward him, hides her face.

He takes her head in his arms, against his heart.

She stays there.

The first sirens roar through S. Thala.

She does not hear them.

The fire grows, spreads.

Through the black smoke, the first flames shoot up, the sky reddens.

With full force all the sirens of S. Thala scream.

She rises. She sees him, hears the sirens, sees the red sky, she does not know where she is. He says:

−It was hot in the room, we came down to the beach.

She remembers, closes her eyes:

−Right . . .

She lies down in his arms once more; against his heart.

•

Someone emerges from the depths of the fire and crosses the beach.

Behind him, S. Thala burns.

He returns. He comes.

He is there.

He sits down a few meters from them, he looks at the sky, the sea.

Throughout S. Thala, unleashed, the terrible sirens.

He looks at the sky, the sea.

Then at her, sleeping in the arms of the traveler.

You hear:

−She's sleeping.

The traveler leans over her sleeping face, says:

−Her eyes seem to be open.

You hear:

−And now day is coming.

The surface of the sea grows pink. Above, the sky loses some color.

You hear:

−Dawn opens her eyes, didn't you know that?
−No.

The traveler watches: her eyes, indeed, are opening more and more, the lids separating, and in a movement so slow it is nearly indiscernible, her whole body follows her eyes, turning toward the growing light.

Stay this way, facing the light.

The traveler asks:

–She sees?

You hear:

–No, she doesn't see anything.

In the night of S. Thala, the sirens wail. The sea swells, loses its color like the sky.

You hear:

–She'll stay just like that until light dawns.

They are silent. The light grows imperceptibly, its movement so slow. Like the separation of sand and water.

The light rises, opens, illuminating the growing space.

The fire fades, like the sky, the sea.

The traveler asks:

–What will happen when the light reaches us?

You hear:

–For an instant it will blind her. Then she will start to see me again. Start to distinguish the sand from the sea, then the sea from the light, then her body from my body. Then she will separate the cold from the night and give it to me. Only then will she hear the sound, you know . . . ? of God? . . . that thing . . . ?

They are silent. They watch the dawning light.

FIN

Afterword
by Sharon Willis

L'Amour forgets. Of course, this is a novel *about* forgetting—and memory. But its narrative presents itself as dispossessed of the very memory that runs through it in the form of recycled figures and images that recall two of Duras's previous novels, *The Ravishing of Lol Stein* (1964) and *The Vice-Consul* (1965). Sometimes known as the "India cycle," this extended text, relayed across three books, performs its own forgetfulness, and imposes a frustrating—even terrifying—amnesia on the reader. But to read *L'Amour* apart from the earlier novels presents another problem, this time more epistemological: without the trans-textual memory that structures and binds these three narratives into one prolonged text, how does *L'Amour* become legible?

Reducing characters to figures as residues, remnants, fragments, this book produces a textual relay that becomes its own internal memory and that dissolves its narrative frame, substituting its memory of the previous texts for the reader's own, implanting memories in us. But like the dead dog on the beach to which *L'Amour* returns with unsettling frequency—as if this corpse structures the narrative space—these are figures in the course of deterioration. Memory is erasing itself. The dead dog, mentioned once in *The Ravishing*, reappears repeatedly in *L'Amour*. Around this dreadful site/ sight, a hole in sense, circulate the unnamed residues of characters that the reader "remembers" from previous texts. Remembering here means fleshing out these haunting ghosts—worn to nubs, "sanded down," to cite the translators—transposed from *The Ravishing* and *The Vice-Consul*: Lol V. Stein, her fiancé, Michael Richardson, and Jacques Hold, the narrator who tells their story while he gradually enters into it.

But instead of grinding to exhaustion in its obsessive return to these figures, this novel relaunches them—translates them—into film, the medium that will preoccupy Duras in the coming years. Haunted by its shape-shifting textual ghosts (in French *revenants*; literally, ones coming back), *L'Amour* also anticipates a cycle of films marked by these same narrative remnants and traces: *La Femme du Gange* (1972), *India Song* (1974), and *Son nom de Venise dans Calcutta désert* (1976). Situated at the joint between the prose cycle and the cinematic one, *L'Amour* produces a site of translation, a space where everything keeps turning into something else. Hence this text's fascination with liminal or threshold spaces: dawn, dusk, the crepuscular. We might even see this space as the place where we can watch this extended novel turning into cinema.

L'Amour is a theater of translation, in which the ongoing conflict between eye and ear, image and speech, stillness and passage, present and past, endlessly mutates. This sense of ceaseless mutation coheres with the persistent boundary failures, between texts, between genres, between textual spaces and between the characters who uneasily inhabit them, that mark Duras's work in general, and that emerge within *L'Amour's* narrative unfolding, troubling its ability even to begin and to end.

In its peculiar textual space, condensation and displacement both remember and refigure the elements and effects that will repeat through the films' repetitions of the characters and images originating in *The Ravishing*. Like S. Thala, the seacoast town where "she," "the man who walks," and "the traveler" circulate through a space they barely map for us, this novel lacks boundaries. "The man who walks gestures at everything, the sea, the beach, the blue town, the white capital, he says: 'Here, this is S. Thala, until the river.' His movement stops. Then his movement resumes, he gestures again, but more precisely, it seems, at all of it, the sea, the beach, the blue town, the white town, towns beyond, others still: all the same. He adds: 'And after the river, that's S. Thala as well'" (11). This passage perfectly condenses *L'Amour's* governing effects.

The staccato textual rhythm produces a strange movement and energy within a limited lexicon, tight repetition, and a paucity of verbs. Like the town, which has expanded beyond all possible boundaries, seeped into everything, *L'Amour* bleeds over any conventional textual—and generic—boundaries. In its carefully rhythmic pacing, this text's prose edges into poetry, but also evokes cinema, as its choppy syntax, continually cut up by punctuation, might suggest a highly dynamic montage of successive reframings. Pace and pacing remain central organizing figures for this text. Its opening passage ends this way: "This man has the even steps [*le pas régulier*] of a prisoner" (4). Later, the traveler observes of the man who walks that "'His path is always the same, his pace so regular, you'd think– '—She shakes her head: no. 'No, it's the rhythm [*le pas*] of this place,' she says. 'The rhythm [*le pas*] of S. Thala'" (14-15). Again and again, we are reminded of rhythm—an echo of poetics and montage—through the word *"pas,"* both the most commonly used negative particle (as in *"ne . . . pas"*) in French and a word for "step" or "pace." This translation does a marvelous job of approximating the rhythm and repetition of *L'Amour*, keeping to short verbs, short sentences, a sense of hesitation and stumbling. Its intent, as the Introduction notes, is to preserve the sense of movement—even agitation, I would say—embedded in its nuanced repetition of verbs in particular. Verbs present a serious challenge to the translators, because many English verbs lack the "spring coil" internal to verbs in French: they contain their own orientation, not relying on prepositions as English does. For example, *revenir*: to come back, *retourner*: to go back; *reculer*: to back up. It's harder, therefore, to capture the edgy and constant motion in the verbs themselves. Moreover, English has two distinct present tense options: simple and progressive. Its progressive emphasizes a process unfolding, and thus temporal movement. French has to imply this, and the present tense of Duras's prose here suggests anything but a smoothly developed unfolding. All this verb activity contributes to the text's tension, like cinema's, between movement and stasis, present and past, stillness and passage.

But this economy of means is not easily attained in English. You want to read *L'Amour* aloud, maybe even more so than most Duras texts, so it is important to preserve the incantatory quality of the syllables in English, which the translators have accomplished masterfully. And the monotonous, almost toneless quality that the French produces carries over into the later film cycle Duras will make, where a near static camera frames the characters while voices off-screen recount their story. Endowed with the resources to achieve the flatness and disembodiment towards which *L'Amour* strives, Duras's films brutally separate voice from body and image.

But equally important, cinema's native tension between stillness and passage—the still photograms hidden under the projected film's flow—echoes the suspended world of *L'Amour*. In an analogous effect, that text's perpetual stalling in a suspended, suspenseful present saturated by its haunting past itself evokes the uncanny coincidence of pastness and presence in cinema's moving images. Cinema, that is, speaks in the present tense, yet each performance of a given film reminds us that, in recording images, the film captures the present's passage into the past.

L'Amour is about suspense—the suspended phrase, the word suspended outside syntax, the suspended look which sees nothing and comes from nowhere. The story begins with the triangle formed by the watching man, the seated woman, and the walking man: "The triangle is completed by the woman with closed eyes . . . The man who watches is between this woman and the man who walks along the edge of the sea. Because of the man who walks, constantly, with his slow, even, stride, the triangle stretches long, reforms, but never breaks" (4). At this scene's "end," "[t]he triangle comes undone, reforms. It comes apart. The man passes. You see him, you hear him. You hear: his pace slacken. The man must be looking at the woman with closed eyes sitting before him. Yes. The steps stop. He looks at her" (5). Together, these characters produce a figure which itself gives way to space. As the step spaces itself, it makes space. Nameless, the male characters, the "he"s, converge and conflate, confusing us: who is looking at whom? But whose gaze frames this scene? Whose voice sustains narration?

What comes on the next page is jarring. First, suspense: "For one moment, no one watches, no one is seen . . . For a moment, no one listens, no one hears. And then there is a cry: the man who was watching closes his eyes, seized by a feeling that lifts him, lifts him up, lifts his face to the sky, his face contorts, and he cries out" (6). Then, after a characteristic spatial break in the text—marked in the translation by "•"—"A cry. Someone cried out over by the sea wall" (6). We are jolted out of the space of our reading. The narrative has migrated from "you" to "no one" to someone unknown. But the "you" has anchored us into an intimate proximity here.

Its effect obliges a detour on translation, since the "you" returns at the end of the text to a similarly uncanny effect. In French, "on" performs multiple pronominal functions: it can mean "one," "we," "people," "you." Its status seems strange from the point of view of English. But I'd argue that there is also a certain estrangement built into its mutability. Since they have to pin it down in English, the translators have made the brilliant choice to use "you," pulling us into a special and uneasy implication in the unfolding scene. The "we" inclusive that "on" allows does as well for the French reading. As "you" gives way abruptly to no one, and to a new voice, we readers are already displaced and disoriented.

Now we have to ask whose voice this is that remains ignorant about what we know from what we've just read? What space does it occupy? "The cry uttered and heard throughout space, whether occupied or empty. It has torn the shadowy light, the stillness. The steps of the man who walks have not stopped, have not slowed" (6). Like the steps, the cry engenders space, but it also tears it apart. And the *récit* itself hangs momentarily suspended on that cry, which reverberates across the three texts of the Lol V. Stein cycle: a delayed cry of grief remains central to *The Ravishing*, and *The Vice-Consul* is structured by the beggar woman's ceaseless cry and the vice consul's single cry that precedes his violent breakdown. Preoccupied by the cry, the barest, most fundamental form of language, the nonspeech of the in-fans, the Lol V. Stein novels, like many of Duras's works, take place *"au bord de la mer"* (by the sea), a phrase that inevitably puns with the word *mère*, mother. Through their obsession with this liminal space, her texts incessantly evoke the preverbal state of contact with the mother. Crucially punctuating all three novels, the cry also represents the point where language begins and fails all at once: pure voice referring to nothing beyond itself.

After the next spatial/typographical break on this same page, we read: "The story. It begins. Began before the walk along the edge of the sea, the cry, the gesture, the movement of the sea, the movement of the light. But now it becomes visible." The story, then, gives itself as an autonomous inscription, in a sentence of its own. But it begins after the text has begun, only to start by telling us that it has already begun, before. It has begun anticipating the cry already emitted. This story has, it seems, in effect, just remembered, only to forget again, its own beginning, its own anteriority. This cry voices the unvoiced cry that marked the end of the ball in *The Ravishing*, arriving after significant delay.

The cry that reframes the narrative figures an insistent textual effect of punctuation and suspension. But this narrative offers no ordinary suspense, and this is its disruptive force, its violence—perhaps—against the novel form itself. This is suspense with no payoff. In this world where no story can fully develop, words refuse reliably to mean; they relinquish referentiality and withdraw into objecthood. For the reader, as for the characters in *L'Amour*, words all too often risk turning into *things*, because they describe nothing, refer to nothing. In this textual space, a reader consistently feels possessed of the same unseeing gaze, the same blind look of the characters.

In this context, it is no accident that the text figures writing itself as a "dead letter," caught and suspended without a trajectory. In the one episode that seems to promise a discrete shape, cohering in a punctual end, the traveler, whom we take to be some iteration of

Michael Richardson, Lol's lost fiancé, composes a letter. "The man takes a piece of paper, he writes: *S. Thala. S. Thala. S. Thala*. He stops. He seems to hesitate between each written word. He begins again. Slowly, with certainty, he writes: *S. Thala, 14 September*. He underlines the first word. Then he writes: *Don't bother coming there's no point*. He pushes the letter away, stands up" (13). The traveler remains himself immobilized, having interrupted the trajectory that his name implies. This letter figures another repetitive mechanism, reflecting its author's automatism. It begins in pure repetition; only on a second try can it inscribe time and place as coordinates. More important, the letter can be pushed away, but not sent. In the last instance of its appearance, when his wife has come to seek him out because she has *not* received his message, we read: "'I wrote to you. The letter is still there.' She puts the letter back on the table" (58). This scene turns on the exchange of the letter as object, on its repositioning, its return to the table. But the moment of reading is elided. This remains a "dead letter," undelivered in its delivery, voided of readable meaning in this couple's encounter: a thing.

In its only other iteration, the second scene of its composition, the letter's figurative quality bodies forth. "He takes up the letter again. He writes. *S. Thala 14 September. Don't come now, don't come, tell the children something, it doesn't matter what*. The hand stops, starts again: *If you can't figure out how to explain it to them, let them make something up*. He puts down the pen, picks it up again: *Regret nothing, nothing, silence all pain, all comprehension, tell yourself that this way you will be as close as possible to* —his hand pauses, starts again, writes: *understanding*. The traveler pushes the letter away" (27).

This scene's inscription of the name, "S. Thala," also figurally marks out its space, a space of offering and taking back, of comings and goings (but no *allers-retours*, since no one quite comes back to their departure point). Its repetition is automatic, the pen hand, posed as independent of the writer, is the agent of writing. Furthermore, this rewriting of the first letter adds nothing, produces no more sense, but merely repeats its negative admonitions. The promise of sense in the narrative pact that binds us is abolished in the destruction of the letter's circuit. When its addressee finally reaches it, in a reversal of conventional postal circuits, she leaves it unread. Condensed to a hard kernel of suspense, the failed exchange of the letter anticipates the text's end. An apparent event, an arson fire, recedes into a mere backdrop for its final scene, the nonevent of two men watching a woman sleep and anticipating the repetition of her waking in the impending daylight.

The letter's full narrative impact occurs at the level of the text's reader. We are aligned with the traveler's wife by the letter's direct address, which recalls the translation's early rendering of the French "on" as "you." Ultimately, the destabilization and displacement that *L'Amour* has wrought strikes the reader's position, implicating our desire in its movement and suspensions. In a way, this text's repetitions work to threaten the space and temporality of readerly desire, to turn us back to our textual memories to supply a forward thrust against its claustrophobic suspense, to fill in the holes rent by its relentless drive to loss.

Translators' Acknowledgments

We are very grateful to Janice Zinser for her incredibly close and careful reading of an earlier draft of the manuscript and the hundreds of comments she provided on matters small and large. We are also thankful to David Young and Shanna Miller McNair, who gave valuable feedback on later drafts of the manuscript.

—KA and LM

Marguerite Duras was born in Giadinh, Vietnam (then Indochina) to French parents. During her lifetime she wrote dozens of plays, film scripts, and novels, including *The Ravishing of Lol Stein*, *The Sea Wall*, and *Hiroshima, Mon Amour*, and was associated with the *nouveau roman* (or new novel) French literary movement. Duras is probably most well known for *The Lover*, an autobiographical work that received the Goncourt prize in 1984 and was made into a film in 1992. She died in Paris in 1996 at the age of 81.

Kazim Ali is a poet, essayist, and novelist. In addition to his own writing he has published a translation of *Water's Footfall* by Sohrab Sepehri. He is also editor of two literary magazines, and teaches Creative Writing and Comparative Literature at Oberlin College as well as the University of Southern Maine.

Libby Murphy teaches courses in modern and contemporary French literature at Oberlin College. She has published articles on print culture and the First World War, and on the reception of Charlie Chaplin's films in wartime and post-war France.

Sharon Willis is Professor of Art History and Visual and Cultural Studies at the University of Rochester, where she teaches courses in film genre, history, and theory. She is the author of *Marguerite Duras: Writing on the Body* and *High Contrast: Race and Gender in Hollywood Films*, and a co-editor of *Camera Obscura*. She has published numerous essays on feminism, cinema, and media.

Open Letter—the University of Rochester's nonprofit, literary translation press—is one of only a handful of publishing houses dedicated to increasing access to world literature for English readers. Publishing ten titles in translation each year, Open Letter searches for works that are extraordinary and influential, works that we hope will become the classics of tomorrow.

Making world literature available in English is crucial to opening our cultural borders, and its availability plays a vital role in maintaining a healthy and vibrant book culture. Open Letter strives to cultivate an audience for these works by helping readers discover imaginative, stunning works of fiction and poetry, and by creating a constellation of international writing that is engaging, stimulating, and enduring.

Current and forthcoming titles from Open Letter include works from Argentina, Bulgaria, Denmark, Germany, Latvia, Netherlands, Poland, Russia, and many other countries.

www.openletterbooks.org